JUNGLE SURVIVOR'S GUIDE

JUNGLE SURVIVOR'S GUIDE

Rory Storm

Illustrated by Mei Lim

SCHOLASTIC INC.
New York Toronto London Auckland Sydney
Mexico City New Delhi Hong Kong Buenos Aires

ISBN 0-439-32856-X

12 11 10 9 8 7 6 5 4 3 2 1 2 3 4 5 6 7/0

Printed in the U.S.A. 40
First Scholastic printing, January 2002

CONTENTS

Chapter One
SO YOU WANNA BE A JUNGLE SURVIVOR?
1

Chapter Two
ARE YOU A JUNGLE SURVIVOR?
8

Chapter Three
BASIC JUNGLE SURVIVAL SKILLS
17

Chapter Four
JUNGLE SURVIVAL STORIES
42

Chapter Five
SURVIVING ANIMAL ATTACKS
58

Chapter Six
MILITARY RESCUES FROM THE JUNGLE
68

Chapter Seven
SAVING LIVES
82

Chapter Eight
WHAT IF . . . ?
95

Chapter Nine
JUNGLE SURVIVOR'S BRAINTEASERS
106

Chapter Ten
YOUR JUNGLE SURVIVOR'S RATING
111

WARNING!

This guide is to learn about extreme survival situations. The techniques are not suitable for use at home and are only to be used in real emergencies.

Rory

SO YOU WANNA BE A JUNGLE SURVIVOR?

SO YOU WANNA BE A JUNGLE SURVIVOR?

Have you ever flown over the treetops of a jungle on your way to your vacation destination and wondered how anyone could ever live there, let alone survive if disaster struck? The jungle stretches as far as the eye can see – an unbroken vista of dense green foliage, dissected by the occasional meandering waterway. Trying to find a lone survivor in that huge, impenetrable expanse would be like trying to find the proverbial needle in a haystack – but trying to find your way out alone? Well, that would surely be impossible, wouldn't it?

AMAZING ESCAPES

I guess it's not absolutely impossible to escape from the jungle, but survival is rare. I have to say that to navigate your way to safety and to travel through this hostile undergrowth is one of the hardest survival tasks I've ever known. It takes great physical fortitude and enormous strength of mind.

My first introduction to this environment was as a young soldier in the hot, sticky, insect-laden jungles of Belize, Central America. I don't mind admitting, I was as jumpy as a cat on hot coals. I felt that eyes were watching me from every bush and that danger lurked around each corner. Of course, I didn't let on to my companions, and we all put on a brave face, but since you can see only 6 feet (1.8 m) in any direction, we all felt panicky and claustrophobic. What a wimpy bunch!

Of course, since then, I've spent many, many hours in the jungle, either alone or with a unit of trusted pals, and I now view this fascinating landscape with great fondness as well as a healthy respect. Yet, I concede that it takes some getting used to.

Most novices in the jungle are somewhat surprised by their nervous reaction. Like all of us, they've read such family classics as *Jungle Book* and *Tarzan* and they expect jungle life to be as it's depicted in the cartoons. However, you soon realize that for the infant Mowgli or Tarzan to be brought up in the jungle by wolves and apes is nothing short of a miracle. Most creatures and plants of the jungle are hell-bent on eating, biting, stinging, or poisoning you. In reality, you have to be exceptionally tough to survive in the humid expanses of the tropical jungle.

GOOD AND BAD

Yet, if survive you must, then in some ways, the jungle is one of the best extreme environments in which to do so. Food is plentiful, with no seasons to create shortages, and there is an abundance of fresh water. This environment even provides you with the materials to make your own shelter and means of transport. A survival paradise, you might think.

But this rosy picture does not take into account the debilitating heat, the virulent tropical diseases, the heaving throng of insect life, and the dangerous wildlife. Nor does it hint at the almost insurmountable difficulties of rescue or escape from the jungle – all of which combine to make even the bravest individual quake with justified trepidation on finding him- or herself alone in the jungle. Many survivors simply go out of their minds!

RESCUE

The difficulty of finding an individual in the jungle is well illustrated by the now celebrated story of 2nd Lt. Hiroo Onada. After going into hiding at the end of the Second World War, he spent 29 years surviving off the land in the jungles of the Philippine island of Lubang. Although several search parties were sent to find him, he always evaded them, believing these overtures to be a trap and that the war was not really over. It was not until 1974, when his original commanding officer returned with an order to surrender that Onada, aged 52, came out.

During his time alone, Onada set snares and traps for game, ate fruit, and occasionally stole livestock from the local farms. Yet he puts his ability to survive and to evade capture for so long down to the fact that he knew the jungles of Lubang better than the locals and could always stay one step ahead.

WHAT TO EXPECT

So, to give you a fighting chance of surviving in the jungles for a fraction of the time Onada spent there, we're going to look at ways to provide yourself with the lifesaving essentials of shelter and water. We'll also explore tactics for dealing with some of the perils that lurk in the depths of the jungle, which can range from crocodile or piranha attacks to dealing with life-sucking leeches and poisonous plants.

Once you've absorbed these basic jungle survivor's skills, you'll have a chance to check out the brave souls who've had to use these techniques for real. And, I'm sure all these tales of derring-do will be just the thing to inspire you to give some ingenious answers to the "What If" scenarios and the Jungle Survivor's Brainteasers, where you can come up with your very own survival plan to save yourself and your friends.

A SILVER LINING

Yet, a good knowledge of survival skills is not enough to ensure successful escape from the jungle. As you'll see from the real-life adventures we recount later, you need determination, resourcefulness, and a belief in your own ability to get you through any jungle ordeal. Perhaps more than any other extreme environment, the jungle messes with your head – so you have to be mentally as well as physically tough to keep believing and to keep going. It's the only way to survive.

Of course, as in all survival situations, you also have to have luck on your side and, preferably, the ability to turn adversity into an advantage. Take, for instance, the story of the fisherman and the forest guard who were out one day on a fishing trip on the Kosi River in the jungles of India. Some might say that it was bad luck for them to find, on turning a bend in the river, that they'd come face-to-face with a man-eating tiger. Others might say that it was doubly unlucky that, while running away from the pursuing tiger, the hapless pair fell over a black bear that was sleeping in a patch of long grass. Well, they might be right. But in the confusion and the shouting, everyone including the tiger and the bear had run in different directions and our pair were able to make their escape. So was that lucky or unlucky, would you say? It depends on the way you look at things, doesn't it. Is the glass half full or half empty?

I hope that you always look on the brighter side of life and that luck will bless you if you ever find yourself in a jungle survival situation.

But, for now, let's settle for narrowing the survival odds in our favor a little by getting down to some jungle survival skills, shall we?

ARE YOU A JUNGLE SURVIVOR?

ARE YOU A JUNGLE SURVIVOR?

If ever you picture yourself in a survival situation, if you're like me, it's most likely to be in the tropics. So, hopefully, you've got some creative ideas tucked up your sleeve about just how you would beat the jungle.

Well, before we start this adventure together – and before you flick on to the nail-biting real-life tales of derring-do – let's see how much you really know, shall we?

But I don't want you to sweat over this questionnaire – it's just a yardstick to gauge how much jungle savvy you have from the outset. Don't worry – just put down the first thing that comes into your head – because by the end of the book, you'll know so much cool survival stuff that I'm sure I'd be happy to come with you on any jungle adventure.

1. How many seasons are there in a rain forest?

A 6
B 4
C 2
D 1

2. A swarm of angry bees attacks you. Should you:

A sit very still
B run through the densest undergrowth you can find
C strip off your clothing and wave it around your head
D try to shoot them

3. The margay lives in the rain forests of Central and South America and is a type of

A cat

B tapir

C monkey

D lemur

4. Rubber trees produce which cash crop?

A latex

B lurex

C rayon

D lycra

5. Groups of African rain forest dwellers distinguished by their small size are known as:

A dwarves

B midgets

C pygmies

D leprechauns

6. In order to escape from the jungle, you have to cross a river. Which spot should you choose to attempt a crossing on foot?

A where the water runs over rocks

B where you can jump in from a nice steep bank

C at the estuary

D where the water is shallowest

7. Your friend is bitten on the calf by a common lancehead snake. Do you

A apply a tourniquet above the bite

B suck out the poison

C put his leg in hot water

D bandage from the knee down to the ankle

8. One of the largest of the jungle predators is the crocodile. It can reach record lengths of up to

A 6 ft (1.8 m)
B 12 ft (3.7 m)
C 18 ft (5.5 m)
D 24 ft (7.3 m)

9. There are two types of jungle, known as primary and secondary jungle. Secondary jungle results from

A an inferiority complex
B clearance of primary jungle for cultivation by man
C forest fires
D the expansion of mangrove swamps

10. The world's largest river is the Amazon. Together with its 1,000 or more tributaries, it holds what percentage of the world's freshwater?

A two-thirds
B half
C a quarter
D an eighth

11. You have to make a shelter in which to sleep in the jungle. The best place is

A at the base of a large dead tree
B by the river
C off the ground
D next to a waterhole

12. Animals living in the canopy of the jungle high above the ground are fine until they have to travel to another treetop. Running down the trunk, across the ground, and up the next is dangerous and a waste of energy. So some animals have developed the ability to travel through the air. The flying tree snake of Southeast Asia can glide through the air to cover distances of up to

A 16.4 ft (5 m)
B 32.8 ft (10 m)
C 65.6 ft (20 m)
D 164 ft (50 m)

ANSWERS

Let's see how you fared with our first dirty dozen, shall we? Give yourself one point for each correct answer.

1d Remarkably, the climate never changes in the rain forest so there are no seasons – the trees can bear flowers and fruits, or shed leaves, at any time of year.

2b The dense foliage should beat off the insects as it springs back – well, that's the theory, anyway. Sitting still, or worse stripping off, is complete madness and you'd have to be a real sharpshooter to pop them off one at a time with a gun!

3a This beautiful cat is nocturnal and has very large eyes to help it see in the dark. All the other animals also live in rain forests.

4a Latex is the sticky sap of a tree that grows in the Amazon. The Indians used it to make waterproof shoes, bottles, and balls to play with, long before settlers realized its value. Lurex, rayon, and lycra are all man-made fibers – sorry, no points there.

5c Pygmies. Many rain forest peoples are short, which may represent a physical adaptation to rain forest life since it's easier to move about in dense undergrowth and to climb trees if you have a small, light frame. Although, admittedly, it rains a lot in Ireland, leprechauns are the mythical "little people" of the Emerald Isle and have never, to my knowledge, been spotted in the jungle.

6d You must choose your spot carefully for wading across rivers. The other three options are all dangerous places to cross because, you want easy access to the water on both sides; water tends to run rapidly over rocks; and estuaries tend to be wide and are prone to awkward tide movements. But never fear, we'll be dealing with river crossings later in the book.

7d This kind of bandaging prevents the toxin from spreading rapidly and being taken up by the lymphatic system. Despite what you see in old Westerns, you should never put a tourniquet on or try to cut or suck out the poison. Placing the wound in cool water is helpful but hot water would simply spread the poison faster.

8c Eighteen feet (5.5 m) of powerful carnivore lunging at you is quite big enough, thank you. But even the smaller crocodiles are powerful enough to overcome large animals – and people – that come down to the rivers in which they live.

9b Yep, secondary jungle is that which has reclaimed an abandoned cultivated area, so instead of tall trees like in primary jungle, there is a mixture of dense undergrowth and creepers, making this kind of jungle more difficult to cross.

10a It's a staggering statistic but it's true. Not only does the Amazon hold two-thirds of the world's freshwater but it supports an incredible diversity of life, including 5,000 species of freshwater fish, and it's believed that there may be as many as 2,000 more yet to be discovered.

11c In the tropics, you definitely want to get off the ground and away from the unpleasant and dangerous creepy crawlies that litter the jungle floor. Insects are abundant by a river, and dead branches can do you serious damage if they drop on you from a height because of a high wind. Unless you want to be flattened by a herd of marauding animals on their way to drink, I suggest you stay well clear of the waterhole.

12d Remarkably, this adaptable reptile raises its ribs upwards and outwards, flattening its body so it can glide from tree to tree. It has been reported to cover an astonishing 164 feet (50 m) – that's more than ten houses stretched end to end!

SCORING

0-4 points:

Tact isn't my strong point, so the less said, the better here I think. Take heart, though, there's plenty of opportunity to polish up your survival know-how later in the book.

5-8 points:

Well, that's a bit more like it. You've obviously got a natural instinct for survival and hopefully we can hone your skills as we progress.

9-12 points:

Bravo! That's an excellent start – pay attention and you should be getting straight A's by the final quiz! But watch out, it's a jungle out there.

Did you survive or were the piranhas snapping at your heels? Whether you're fish bait or a survival champ, there's always more to learn, so what are you waiting for?

Let's pack our survival kits and get going!

BASIC JUNGLE SURVIVAL SKILLS

BASIC JUNGLE SURVIVAL SKILLS

I hate to say it, but some pretty awful misadventure has probably befallen you, if you find yourself alone in a survival situation in the jungle. It's only natural to feel more than a bit shaken up, but if you are to make it through your ordeal, you must try to stay calm and think carefully about what you need to survive.

Your first priority is somewhere safe to sleep for the night, because the jungle is full of creatures that can give you anything from a nasty nip to a deadly bite or sting. So, let's take a closer look at constructing yourself a shelter and bed before we move on to the other survival essentials.

MAKING A JUNGLE SHELTER

Wood is plentiful in the jungle, so as long as you've got a machete, ax, or knife with you (all essential items in a jungle survival pack), you should have no problem making a comfortable place to rest.

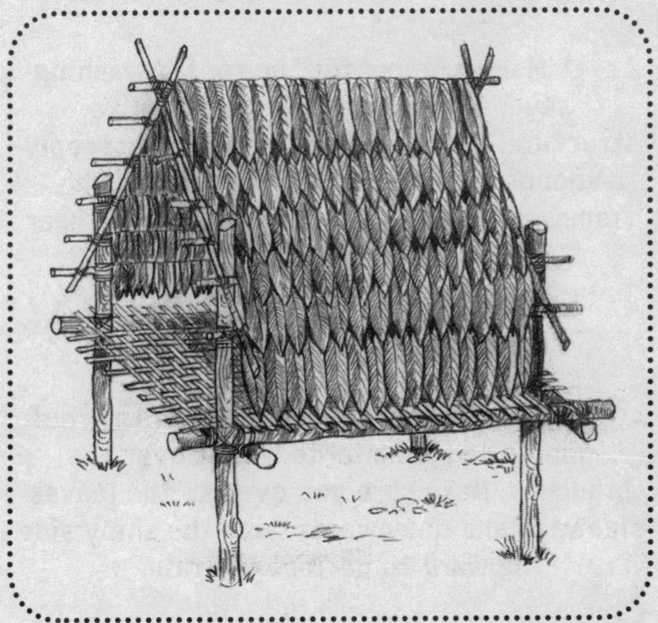

- Either find four trees in a rectangle or drive four logs that are a little taller than you into the ground, in a square formation.
- Lash some branches (cross poles) across at both ends and two branches between the posts – lash them into notches cut on the outsides of the posts, to make a bed frame.
- Either weave smaller branches across the frame or lay cross bars all the way along the bed and cover with leaves and/or grass.

- Make a frame for the roof by lashing seven poles together in a tentlike structure. The roof must be pitched steeply enough for the rain to run off, and the framework should be strong enough to bear the weight of the thatch.

- Lash the roof to the vertical corner poles.

- Lash more branches between the roof gables and hang large leaves over the branches. Make sure you overlap the leaves sideways and downwards with the shiny side upward to deflect the rain.

Jungle Survivor's Tip

Make sure the bed is large enough to hold both you and your equipment.

Jungle Survivor's Tip

SAS and Gurkha soldiers always take two sets of clothes on operational patrols. They change into a dry set, which they've kept in a backpack, to sleep in at night and then put the damp set back on in the morning. The change is uncomfortable but you're going to be wet inside a few minutes anyway — and this guarantees you a good night's sleep.

BAMBOO SHELTER

Bamboo is plentiful in tropical or semitropical regions and it is a great building material for making shelters.

Set four thick, straight posts into the ground. In length, they should be roughly your height plus a little. (The front posts should be shorter than the back posts with a forked bit to hold the gutter. With the front posts lower than the back, the roof will slope and the rain will run off.)

Place long branches between the upright posts.

Using a knife, split a bamboo stem lengthways and lay it between the shorter front uprights to form a kind of gutter. Block one end with leaves or stones and put a pot under the other end to catch rainwater as it runs off the roof. You might as well get something for nothing if you can. (See next page for diagram.)

Now for the roof itself!

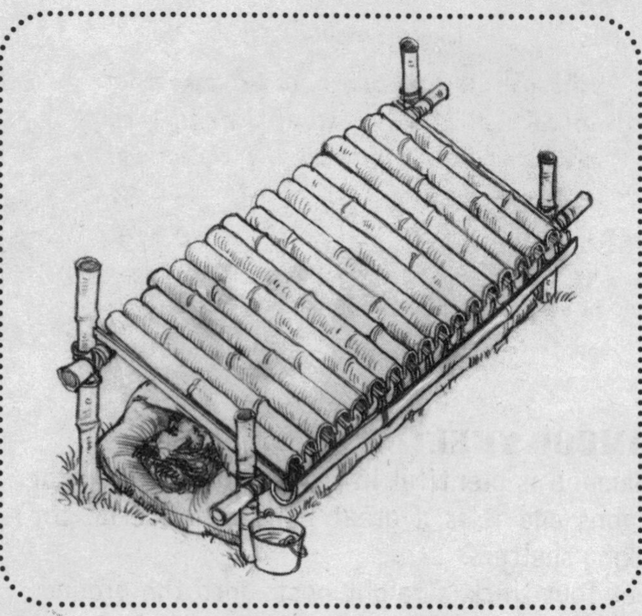

Lay split bamboo stems between the ridgepoles, open sides up. Rest the bottom of them in the gutter itself.

Now place more stems on top, this time with the round side uppermost, so that the top layer interlocks with the bottom layer (see diagram).

CAUTION: Take great care when working with bamboo. It is easy to split but the resulting splinters are razor-sharp. Bamboo shoots also have fine, stinging hairs at the base, which should be avoided. Finally, clumps of bamboo stems are often under great tension and may suddenly shatter or whiplash back at you when you cut them, so be very careful.

Fact File
Giant bamboos grow at an impressive rate – up to 9 inches (23 cm) in a day and can reach a height of 80 feet (24.4 m).

MAKING A FIRE

Now that you have somewhere to shelter from the downpours and a comfortable place to sleep, you should turn your attention to a fire.

In the tropics, a fire is primarily for cooking and water purification rather than a source of heat. You will have no problems finding fuel but much of it is permanently damp, so be selective. Make sure you find some good dry tinder and keep it safe in your shelter or backpack to stay dry – if you stick it inside your shirt, it'll soon be soaked in sweat during the heat of the day!

You may use your fire for cooking and for purifying water by boiling it, but it also serves another very useful purpose. Can you guess? Well, the smoke from a fire is a very efficient way to fend off insect pests, especially mosquitoes. Did you get that?

If the ground is very wet (and it probably will be), then build your fire on a platform – you can use cut green branches covered in mud.

Jungle Survivor's Tip

A Good Night's Sleep

- Don't camp close to swamps, dry watercourses, or animal trails.
- Choose high ground whenever possible.
- Before clearing the ground, check vegetation for snakes and insects.
- Check the trees above for rotten branches, fallen trees that are resting against others, known as "hang-ups," and wildlife. If present, avoid these places since "hang-ups" alone cause numerous deaths in the jungle.
- Make sure your bed is above the ground – a hammock is ideal and can be improvised from a parachute if you don't have a hammock. A hammock has the added advantage that it can be built on a slope just as easily as on flat ground!
- A tree house is easier to make than it sounds.
- Use what is available – if your aircraft has crash-landed in the jungle, use a section as a shelter (removing seats to make space for sleeping).
- If you can find it, mosquito netting will make your life a lot more comfortable.

Jungle Survivor's Tip

While flying insects stay away from the smoke of a fire, crawling insects don't like walking over ash, either, so it's a good idea to spread some cooled ash around your sleeping area at night. It's amazing what you can do with a fire, isn't it!

FINDING WATER

Water, water everywhere and not a drop to drink. So lamented that salty old sea dog, the Ancient Mariner, but it's a lot like that in the jungle, too. There's certainly no shortage of water but it's full of potential dangers and, no matter how thirsty you're feeling, you should observe a few sensible precautions before you start slurping it up from streams and plants, etc.

Sad to say, bad water can kill more quickly and painfully than no water at all, so assume that all jungle water other than direct rainfall is contaminated with bacteria, viruses, and parasites and always purify it before drinking.

JUNGLE PLANTS

Many jungle plants act as water containers, catching rain and moisture in the atmosphere. These are a ready source of water – check hollow old bamboo stems by shaking to see if you can hear any water sloshing around inside. If so, pierce the stem carefully just above each joint and catch the water as it pours out.

Similarly, the pitcher plant is worth looking out for – its leaves form a natural "reservoir," which fills with water to trap small insects, leeches, etc. This is easily collected but must be filtered and purified before drinking unless you like something chewy as you swallow.

Some plants have a high water content and can be used as an emergency supply or when traveling. Vines, in particular, offer a good supply of freshwater and here's a good tip for getting a free drink quickly and easily in the jungle:

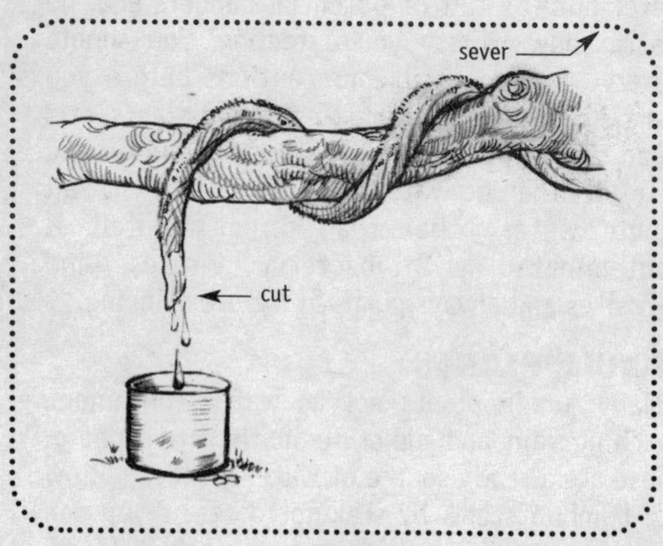

- Cut deeply into the vine as high up as you can reach.
- Then sever the vine completely near to the ground.

CAUTION: I've always found the freshwater from vines to be lovely and clear and sweet but if it's at all murky or causes the slightest irritation in your mouth, stop immediately – this could indicate poison. Choose another vine.

- The water flows upwards through capillary action and will drip from the highest cut end into a container (or your mouth if you don't have one).

Jungle Survivor's Tip

Bamboo segments make a great water container — cut a thick bamboo stem about 1 inch (2.5 cm) below a segment ring and the same distance below the next ring down. This will give you a hollow container with an open top — just the ticket!

PURIFYING WATER

The best way to purify suspicious water is:

- Boil it for at least three minutes.
- Use water-sterilizing tablets, if you have them.
- Filter water to remove dead insects, etc. – a finely woven material such as muslin or mosquito netting is best but even a sock will do (smelly, but necessity rules in a survival situation!).
- Muddy water can be strained through a sand-filled cloth or a bamboo pipe filled with leaves and/or grass – then boiled.
- Don't drink directly from streams, but collect and purify it as above.

Jungle Survivor's Tip

Stretch out some waterproof sheeting and attach between several trees in a tropical downpour and you can collect yourself as much as 3-4 quarts (3-4 l) of drinkable water in a matter of ten minutes or so. Nice work if you can get it!

FINDING FOOD

Although food is abundant in the tropics, you should still take the usual care with potentially poisonous plants.

The best places to forage will be along streams and watercourses – in fact, anywhere where the sun can penetrate to ripen the fruit.

Because there is so much readily available food and because some of it is poisonous, only eat foods that you recognize from their cultivated varieties such as bananas and avocados which, incidentally, are a favorite food of jaguars, so watch out for fellow diners! Even eating foods you recognize, you must exercise discretion – for example, a plant that we get strychnine from has fruits that look like oranges but which are deadly poisonous. If in doubt, or if you need to eat unknown plants, always apply the edibility test using tiny amounts:

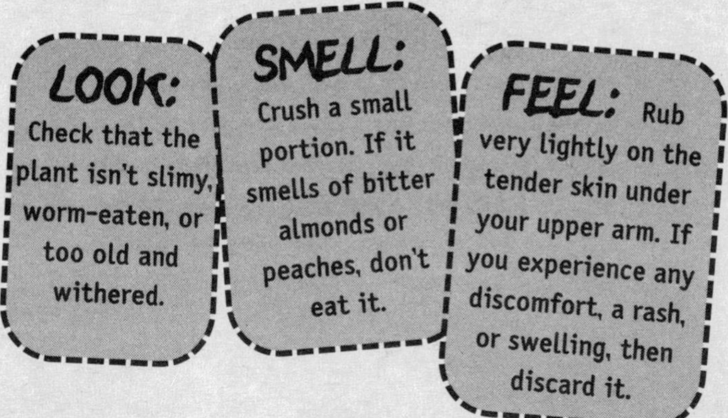

TASTE: So far, so good. Now, try the next routine, leaving a fifteen-second reaction time between each step:

- Place a small portion on the lips
- Place a small portion in the corner of your mouth
- Place a small portion on tip of tongue
- Place a small portion under tongue
- Chew a small portion
- If at any time you experience any discomfort, discard it.

SAMPLE: Swallow a very small amount and wait five hours. Don't eat or drink anything else during this time. If no reactions are experienced, you can consider the plant safe to eat.

Fact File

Gurkha soldiers pick as they walk when in the jungle. They pop the goodies into a net on the back of their bergens (backpacks) so they have fresh fruit and vegetables with dinner!

Jungle Survivor's Tip

There's a plant that grows in the jungle that is respectfully known as "wait-awhile." Can you guess why? Well, it earned its name because if you get snagged up on its vicious thorns you have no choice but to wait for your friends to disentangle you. If you're alone, walk backwards to free yourself from its fierce clutches and then go around. Never try to press on through wait-awhile or you'll wind up with your clothes in tatters and no skin!

JUNGLE TRAVEL

In most situations in which your plane crash-lands or your vehicle breaks down, you are advised to stay with the vehicle because rescuers can find that more easily than finding you. However, in the jungle, unless it's a huge commercial airplane that came down, leaving an easily identifiable swath through the forest, a small crashed plane or broken-down vehicle is hidden from the sky by the dense foliage and canopy, so your chances of rescue are severely handicapped.

Therefore, you should choose to stay put in the jungle only if you are sure that somebody knows of your plight and your position and has the resources to rescue you. Otherwise, your best option is to walk out. Jungle travel is demanding and painstaking and it could take days or even months – so you'd better polish up on your survival skills while you can.

BEFORE YOU SET OFF

If you are going to travel through the jungle, you should prepare yourself as best you can. Despite the heat, cover up your arms and legs with clothing as much as possible to prevent cuts and scratches. A hat with a brim can keep vegetation away from the eyes, and if you have it, insect repellent should be liberally splashed over all exposed skin except the forehead – you don't want it running into your eyes with the sweat because it's not very pleasant, I can tell you!

Keep your machete or knife sheathed unless you need it and carry plenty of water – the humidity and sheer exertion of jungle travel makes heat exhaustion a constant threat, so you must drink regularly.

Jungle Survivor's Tip

If you're really smart, you'll drape some mosquito netting over your hat and tuck it into your shirt when you're making camp at dusk. This keeps the swarms of mosquitoes out of your mouth, ears, and eyes and affords you a modicum of protection. Unfortunately, the mesh is too fine to use when you're traveling but at least the mosquitoes aren't such a nuisance during the heat of the day.

Jungle Survivor's Tip

If you have access to a first aid kit, bandages are invaluable. Keep small punctures and cuts covered to avoid the infections that are commonplace in the tropics.

MOVING THROUGH THE JUNGLE

In a primary jungle, trees can grow 200 feet (60 m) tall and the dense canopy means that the jungle floor remains relatively free of vegetation. So traveling through primary jungle is relatively easy but a secondary jungle (where vegetation has grown back once people have cut down the trees) is dense and very difficult to negotiate.

Cutting a path is slow and exhausting and progress through this sort of terrain is normally slowed to about 3 miles (5 km) a day. That may not seem like much but, believe me, you'll be exhausted by the end of it.

So here are some tips on how to move through this impenetrable terrain:

- **Don't fight the jungle, think laterally.**
- **Don't try to follow a compass bearing rigidly – it's not worth the effort.**
- **Instead, seek areas of thinner vegetation, native paths, game trails, dry watercourses, streams, etc. that lead roughly in the right direction.**
- **Follow ridge tops where possible.**
- **Move slowly, stopping regularly to orient yourself and to drink water.**

Stop regularly to remove parasites such as leeches and chiggers (chigoes) – if left for any length of time, they can cause infection.

Don't travel after sunset when predators will be out and about looking for an easy meal – i.e., you.

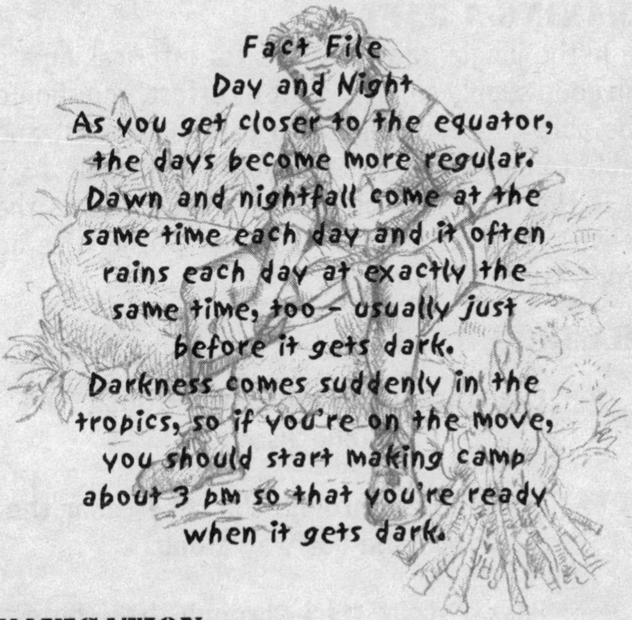

Fact File
Day and Night
As you get closer to the equator, the days become more regular. Dawn and nightfall come at the same time each day and it often rains each day at exactly the same time, too – usually just before it gets dark.
Darkness comes suddenly in the tropics, so if you're on the move, you should start making camp about 3 pm so that you're ready when it gets dark.

NAVIGATION

As a jungle survivor, you can use the travel tips mentioned above to help you walk out. But remember to stay smart about it – you're not going to cover much ground on foot unless you find a man-made track that may link villages or a logging track that should also lead you to help.

The other way to cover ground more quickly is to build a raft and let the river do the work! Obviously, this faster mode of transport is not without its hazards – dangerous animals and waters spring to mind, but it is faster than hacking your way through dense jungle.

MAKING A RAFT

In the jungle, raw materials for raft-making are in good supply so, with a bit of effort, you should be able to make something that is buoyant and able to carry both you and your equipment.

If there's plenty of bamboo about, this is the easiest raft to make in the jungle, otherwise go for a traditional log raft.

BAMBOO RAFT

- **Cut thickish bamboo in 10-foot (3-m) lengths.**
- **Make holes through the canes near the ends and halfway along.**
- **Pass a stout stick through these holes to connect the bamboo.**
- **Lash each of the bamboo canes to the sticks with twine, rattan, or other vines.**

- Make a second deck in the same way (one deck will not be stable enough to support your weight) and fit it on top of the first.

- Lash the two together, and presto, you're ready to launch.

Jungle Survivor's Tip

Secure all your equipment to the raft with ropes or vines.

GRIPPER BAR RAFT

Cut some timber to form logs for the deck of your raft. Choose leaning trees because these are easiest to drop and to predict where they'll fall.

You will also need four thickish branches with some pliability that are long enough to overlap the width of your deck.

Make notches at each end of the "gripper" branches to stop the ropes from slipping.

Place two branches on the ground and lay the logs out on top of them.

Place the remaining two branches on top and tie each pair of branches firmly together on one side.

Now, with the help of a friend, or lying on top of the gripper to force the opposite ends together, tie the remaining ends so that the logs are gripped tightly between the grippers.

Keep the knots at the top of the deck so you can adjust and tighten the lashings as necessary. If you have time, you can also lash each of the logs together for good measure.

Jungle Survivor's Tip

If possible, test the raft in shallow water before launching it on a deep river.

MAKING A PADDLE

A paddle can act as a rudder so you can steer your raft to safety.

Strip the stems from a strong, green branch, using your knife.

Cut a wedge shape at one end.

Tie two shorter, straight sticks on either side of the wedged end.

Lash a third piece of wood into the center gap against the wedge shape to make the blade of the paddle.

Check the lashings regularly once wet, as they may need tightening.

LAUNCHING AND STEERING

Build your raft close to the water in case it's too heavy to carry to the bank.

Secure the raft to a tree or rock before launching so you can load it once it's in the water.

Load the equipment evenly and in the center of the raft for the greatest stability.

When loaded, some rafts float just below the surface of the water. Don't worry, you may get your feet wet but it should be safe enough.

Use your paddle as a rudder to steer the raft as well as to propel you down the river.

If you want to stand up to steer, you'll have to lengthen the handle of your paddle by lashing a long branch to it.

Remember that a raft turns relatively slowly, so make allowances when steering.

Try to avoid crashing into the bank or large objects because this will wreck the raft quicker than anything.

SIGNALING

Although in most cases it is best to try and walk out of the jungle unless your location is known, if you or one of your party are injured, this may not be possible. In this situation you will have to let potential rescuers know your whereabouts.

The very best way to do this is by a radio rescue beacon or radar-reflective balloon, but if you don't happen to have one of those on you, then you'll have to improvise.

The sheer density of the jungle canopy means that the smoke from signal fires cannot be seen and that you will not hear a rescue aircraft until it is virtually on top of you. So, you're better off making some kind of permanent signal. The aircraft or parachute itself can do this job if it's still stuck up in the canopy. Failing this, lay out some ground signals, but make sure it's somewhere that can be seen from the sky.

A rescue aircraft will be checking every clearing and along riverbanks that are normally visible from the air. If you're close to a river, make full use of it. There may be small islands that are large enough to hold a signal fire (make sure you can hop across to it pretty quickly because you won't get a lot of warning from engine sound, which is muffled in the jungle). Alternatively, you could make yourself a small raft and use it as a fire platform. Tether it to the bank and, when needed, light your fire and push it into midstream where it stands a good chance of being spotted. If you can't make a fire, use any conspicuous permanent signal on these prominent places.

Fact File

Rescuing survivors from the jungle is particularly difficult and perilous, as you'll see in following chapters. Ground searches are rare because of the difficulty in finding something as small as an aircraft, let alone a person, in the vastness of the tropical forest. It is also very difficult to extract a survivor by helicopter because of the denseness of the canopy. If you hope to be found and picked up, you'll increase your chances if you manage to get yourself to a clearing of some sort.

JUNGLE SURVIVAL STORIES

JUNGLE SURVIVAL STORIES

Think you have all that useful information filed away in your little gray cells? Well, while you're storing it up for future use, why don't we take a look at a few remarkable people who have had to put the theory to the test?

All of the following survivors had to rely on their ingenuity, courage, and will to survive. As you read, you can marvel at their fortitude and you might like to imagine just how you might have reacted in the same situation.

CHRISTMAS IN HELL

On Christmas Eve, 1971, a passenger plane took off on a flight from Lima, the capital of Peru, to Pucallpa, some 475 miles (764 km) east in the Peruvian jungle.

Less than half an hour from its destination, the aircraft ran into a violent storm and radio contact with the ground was lost. Unbeknown to air traffic control, the plane had broken up in midair and the ninety-two passengers and crew had plummeted to the ground.

Juliane Koepcke, a seventeen-year-old German girl, was traveling with her mother on the ill-fated flight that day, and she was the only passenger to come out of the jungle alive.

DEATH-DEFYING FALL

When the plane broke up, Juliane fell 10,000 feet (3,048 m), still strapped in her seat, to the jungle below. Miraculously, she only broke her collarbone and slashed her arms and legs in the fall, although she was knocked unconscious. It was an amazing escape but Juliane's nightmare was only just beginning.

When Juliane came around, she realized she was lying in a row of seats that was upside down. Her shoes and glasses were missing. She stayed like this throughout the night, drifting in and out of consciousness.

On Christmas morning, she woke up and started to search for her mother. Not the best of Christmas presents, was it? During her quest, she found a small bag of sweets and a Christmas cake, but that was all. The cake was wet and inedible but the sweets were to become her only sustenance for the next few days of her ordeal.

SO CLOSE YET SO FAR AWAY

Juliane could hear the search planes and helicopters overhead but they couldn't see the wreckage in the dense jungle.

She came across a row of seats with the dead bodies still strapped in. Gingerly, she moved the passengers' feet with a long stick – both female bodies had painted toenails, something her mother never did. So she still had some hope left.

Armed with her long stick, she set off to find a stream or river – advice her parents had given her some years before. Would you have stayed calm and remembered your survival skills in the heat of the moment like that?

HORRENDOUS INJURIES

By now, she was covered in insect bites. One blowfly bite on her arm had developed into a deep and painful hole, full of maggots. She tried to get them out with a small stick but it was in a difficult place and she was largely unsuccessful.

It was now two days since the crash and Juliane was following a small stream that twisted and meandered through the jungle. She followed the bank but progress was slow. She was worried that if she swam, the blood from her wounds might attract an attack by piranhas or crocodiles.

Again, she came across seats from the plane holding bodies but there were no other survivors. Juliane simply had to press on.

On the third day, a search aircraft came frustratingly close. Juliane couldn't stop herself from calling out, but the plane flew on without seeing her. Would you have despaired and given up at this point or would you have the fortitude to carry on?

GRIM DETERMINATION

By the fourth day, her supply of sweets was exhausted and her whole body was swollen from the bites of mosquitoes and blowflies. However, her hopes were raised slightly when the stream she had been following ran into a bigger river, and she knew her chances of coming across civilization were increased.

For five more days, she alternately swam and walked downstream, the image of seeing her father again driving her on. Yet, without food and in the humid heat of 113°F (45°C), she was getting weaker all the time. The maggots feasting on her open wounds didn't help matters any and Juliane feared that they would have to amputate her arm if she ever reached safety.

Although she saw lots of delicious-looking fruits, Juliane didn't eat any because she knew that many things in the jungle look beautiful but are, in fact, poisonous. Despite this, she claims that she wasn't hungry during her ordeal.

SIGNS OF LIFE

By now, the river was widening and the current was so swift that she no longer had the strength to swim in it.

At last, late in the afternoon of the 9th day after the crash, as she looked for somewhere to lie down for the night, Juliane spotted a canoe moored on the riverbank. Nearby was a hut. Inside, she found a small outboard motor together with a can of gasoline and a bag of salt.

Juliane poured the gasoline into the wounds where the maggots were. It hurt ferociously as the maggots tried to bite their way out . . .

The next morning, she reasoned that it might be weeks before the boat owners returned and she prepared to set off again. Remarkably, she didn't consider taking the boat because she knew it belonged to someone else. However, it was raining so hard that she stayed in the hut.

DISCOVERED AT LAST

Late that afternoon, two rain-soaked woodcutters, Amado Pereyra and Marcio Ribera, turned up at the hut and stumbled across Juliane. Her eyes were completely bloodshot, her arms and legs were ravaged by maggot holes, and her face was swollen and disfigured by insect bites.

The two men helped to pick the maggots from her flesh and then took her in the boat to an agricultural colony at Tournavista, from where she was flown to a doctor at Pucallpa. There, she was reunited with her father.

While she was in the jungle, Juliane had managed to walk but as soon as she got to a doctor, her leg went rigid. It turned out that she had a badly torn ligament in her knee, and she should not have been able to walk at all. How's that for mind over body!

Juliane gave rescuers directions, and the search planes located the wreckage spread over 10,000 feet (3,048 m) of jungle.

Juliane's survival was miraculous for several reasons. Not only did she survive the 10,000-foot fall, but the woodcutters who found her only go to the hut once every three weeks. Moreover, had she set off downstream again on foot as she'd planned, she might never have left the jungle alive because it becomes impenetrable a little further downstream and there were no settlements that she could have reached for many days.

Luck was definitely on Juliane's side but it was grim determination, courage, and self-belief that got her through her ordeal.

Fact File

It may sound gross, but in the days of yore, maggots and leeches were actually used by medical staff to treat wounds and, believe it or not, they are being reintroduced by doctors today.

Maggots were put into messy wounds to eat away the dead flesh and then removed. This was an anti-gangrene treatment. And leeches were used to "let blood."

Now, because of the anticoagulant properties in their saliva, which prevents blood from clotting, leeches are being used in microsurgery where incisions must stay open and free-flowing during surgery.

LOST AND FOUND

In 1982, Yossi Ghinsberg, a young Israeli backpacker, was several months into his grand tour of South America when he arrived in La Paz, capital of Bolivia.

Here, he fell into company with two other travelers and an Austrian expatriate named Karl, who described himself as a gold miner, jaguar hunter, and jungle expert. For a fee, Karl agreed to guide the three gringos to a remote Indian village in the jungle and to the Tuichi River where, he alleged, gold could be found.

A few days later, with a couple of bootleg rifles and a few bags of rice, the four of them took a bush plane over the Andes to the verdant upper Amazon basin.

THE TRAIL GOES COLD

However, after several weeks of arduous trekking through the jungle, the three backpackers were beginning to doubt Karl's credentials. The Indian village – and for that matter, the rich gold sites – never materialized.

Tired and demoralized, they backtracked to their starting point where they bought a balsa-log raft from the locals. This time, the plan was to float down the swift-flowing Tuichi to the airfield at Rurrenabaque.

Little did they realize that the river was, if possible, even more treacherous than the jungle. As soon as they set out, it became obvious that the raft was not up to the white water of the river. After two days of terror, the group split up. Karl, the guide, and a young Swiss guy called Marcus refused to go on. The party shared out the provisions and these two started back upriver on foot. Neither was ever seen again. So what do you reckon – would you have turned back or would you have pressed on into the unknown? A hard call, isn't it?

CHURNING HELLHOLE

Yossi and Kevin Gale, an American, set off again on the raft. However, danger lay around the first bend. Before they knew it, the river had constricted and sheer rock walls rose up on either side. The speed and force of the water was formidable as they raced towards the infamous and un-runnable churning cauldron known as San Pedro Canyon.

The raft crashed into a large rock and was held there by the relentless current. At this point, Kevin managed to jump off and, miraculously, made it to the shore. Yossi, on the other hand, was less fortunate. He clung desperately to the flimsy raft as it gradually worked free and then promptly plummeted over a waterfall into the canyon below. For an eternity, Yossi was pinned under the crushing volume of water crashing down on him, but he eventually washed up a mile further on a narrow gravel beach. He was gasping for breath, battered, and completely alone.

TRIAL BY ORDEAL

Over the next 20 days, Yossi Ghinsberg wandered in the deep jungle in search of a trail, food, and ultimately help. During his three-week ordeal, he was tormented by a catalogue of disasters that threatened to finish him off but still he kept going.

Could you have continued if you'd woken up covered in leeches from head to foot? How about if you'd slipped down a slope and got a sharp stick impaled in your bottom? Not a nice thought, is it? One day, Yossi sank up to his chest in quicksand. Luckily, he managed to escape, only to do the very same thing again the next day! Could you have carried on after not one but two near misses in the quicksand? What about the night Yossi was so exhausted that he wet himself – he awoke the next morning to find that not only was a swarm of termites devouring his salty clothes, but huge patches of his skin, too? Or waking up with a jaguar breathing in your face? Yossi didn't know who was the more surprised by his screams.

All these torments were enough to make a lesser soul roll over and die. But Yossi was made of sterner stuff than that. After nearly three weeks alone in the rain forests, Yossi heard the drone of an outboard motor and, music to his ears, someone was calling his name. Can you believe it? It was his friend Kevin who'd come looking for him guided by a riverman called Tico Tudela. Yossi was rescued.

Isn't that the most amazing adventure ever?

Jungle Survivor's Tip

If, like Yossi Ghinsberg, you find yourself in quicksand, here's what you should do! Spread your arms and legs wide and try to float on your back to escape the deadly clutches of quicksand.

If you have a long walking stick with you, lay it on the surface of the quicksand (any pole or stout stick will do).

Lay on your back on top of the walking stick. After a short while, you should stop sinking and start to float.

Once you've stopped sinking, work the stick so it's at right angles to your backbone

and try to get it under your hips. Once your hips are over the pole, you can very slowly start to pull out one leg and then the other.

Get to firmer ground by the shortest route possible, but don't panic and rush or you'll sink again. Take your time.

If you are not alone, another person can lie at the edge of the quicksand, pass you the end of a long branch, and pull you out. Lean on your backpack to spread your weight.

In any event, try not to panic or struggle — sudden movement only stirs up the surface and causes you to sink faster!

MAPPING UNCHARTED TERRITORY

Long before Yossi Ghinsberg underwent his amazing adventure down the Tuichi River, there was another intrepid adventurer meeting challenges in Bolivia.

In 1906, the Royal Geographical Society commissioned Colonel Percy Fawcett to complete a boundary survey of the country, since borders between Bolivia and neighboring Brazil were uncharted.

Fawcett faced huge logistical problems in simply getting his large expedition through the jungle to achieve its objectives. However, he was fascinated by the region and returned time and time again to chart this hostile land.

UNFRIENDLY LOCALS

In 1910, Fawcett and his group were venturing up the Heath River. The tribes along the Heath had a reputation for unrestrained savagery but Fawcett believed that if you treated the Indians with kindness, you would receive benevolence in return. Little did he realize that he was about to be given a chance to put his theory to the test.

After a week paddling upstream, the party turned a bend and came face-to-face with an Indian encampment on a sandbar. Both parties were equally surprised and, momentarily, pandemonium ensued. The natives hurriedly gathered up their children and hid in the trees while the expedition grounded their canoes on the sandbar.

Arrows started to whiz by the men's ears and land in the sand around them. Fawcett attempted to make peace with a few native words but the message fell on deaf ears and the arrows continued to fly.

He then had an idea. Crazy as it sounds, he asked one of his group who was seated just out of arrow range to play his accordion. As the arrows rained down, the man sang some popular classics such as "A Bicycle Built for Two" and "Onward Christian Soldiers," until finally he changed the lyrics to "they've-all-stopped-shooting-at-us." He was right!

Fawcett then approached the natives and exchanged gifts as a sign of friendship. An unorthodox approach, you might think, but it worked.

However, some encounters didn't turn out so well. On one occasion, during a trip down the Chocolate River, the pilot of Fawcett's boat was sent off to inspect a nearby road. After a long delay, Fawcett went to investigate and found the poor man dead with forty-two arrows in his body.

ANIMAL ENCOUNTERS

During his travels, Fawcett had many run-ins with dangerous animals in the jungle. Vampire bats proved to be a particularly unpleasant nuisance and once, as the Colonel was climbing into his sleeping bag, he felt something large and hairy scuttle up his arm and over his neck. It was a gigantic apazauca spider. Fawcett tried to shake it off but the spider hung on fiercely. After much frantic hopping about, the spider dropped to the ground and walked away without attacking – luckily for Fawcett, because the apazauca's bite is poisonous and can be fatal.

Poisonous snakes attacked members of his party and one man lost two fingers as he was washing his bloodstained hands in the river – they were bitten off by piranhas!

FINAL ADVENTURE

Colonel Fawcett had survived many adventures in the jungle including his raft going over a 20-foot (6-m) waterfall and near starvation when his party went without food for over 20 days in a polluted and deserted part of the jungle.

He returned to England to serve in World War I, but the Colonel couldn't stay away from the South American jungle for long.

In 1925, he set out again – this time, to discover an ancient city concealed in the wilds of Brazil. He was accompanied by his son, Jack, and one of Jack's friends. Fawcett left word that should they not return, a rescue expedition was not be mounted because he considered it too dangerous.

On May 29, 1925, Fawcett sent a message to his wife telling her that they were ready to enter unexplored territory. The three explorers sent back the assistants who had helped them thus far and set off alone. Fawcett said in his note, "You need have no fear of failure . . ." These were the last words received from the group. They disappeared into the jungle and were never seen again.

Despite his wishes, several rescue attempts were mounted without success. In 1996, a modern expedition was put together to look for traces of Fawcett but it didn't get very far. Indians kidnapped the party and threatened their lives. They were finally released unharmed but the Indians kept all their valuable equipment.

It seems that even seventy years after his disappearance, the jungle is far too dangerous for anyone to follow in Colonel Percy Fawcett's footsteps!

SURVIVING ANIMAL ATTACKS

SURVIVING ANIMAL ATTACKS

In the minds of jungle survivors, every rustle, every snuffle, and every howl turns into a ferocious, slavering beast about to pounce. In truth, attacks by large predators are relatively rare and it's the itsy-bitsy insect life, such as malaria-carrying mosquitoes, that poses the biggest dangers.

Nonetheless, big cats, snakes, and crocodiles have all, on occasion, been known to attack people, and these survivors' accounts give you some idea of just how terrifying it must be to endure a frenzied attack.

THE MAN-EATING TIGER OF CHOWGARH

In the 1920s, a famous hunter called Jim Corbett was called on by the Indian authorities to kill several tigers who had turned into man-eaters and who were menacing the local populations.

Very few people who were attacked by tigers in the hilly jungles of the Kumaon region ever lived to tell the tale. However, Corbett met one man who had a remarkable escape.

This particular villager, who happened by good fortune to be the biggest and strongest man in the region, was cutting grass with his 8-year-old son on a steep bank near his home, just below the edge of the jungle.

As he stopped to tie the grass into a big bundle, the tiger crept from the trees and sprang at him. It sank its teeth into his head – one under his right eye, one in his chin, and two at the back of his neck!

The tiger struck him with such force that he fell onto his back, and the tiger lay on top of him, chest to chest. As he fell backwards, his out-flung hand touched an oak sapling.

SUPERHUMAN EFFORT

Instantly, the man had an idea that might just save him – remote though the chances were. The pain, as the tiger crushed all the bones on the right side of his face, was terrible but remarkably, the man did not lose consciousness. He very gingerly, so as not to anger the tiger, brought his legs up on either side of it and gently inserted his bare feet against its belly. Simultaneously, he put his left arm under its chest and gave an almighty heave.

Amazingly, he managed to lift the tiger right off the ground and, being on the very edge of the perpendicular hillside, the tiger went crashing down through the jungle trees. If he hadn't been holding tightly to the sapling, the villager would have been dragged down with the tiger.

REMARKABLE RECOVERY

The man's son ran up to his injured father and wrapped his terrible wounds in a loincloth and

CHAPTER FIVE

Fact File

You are much less likely to be attacked by wild animals than you might think. Even predators tend to be scared of humans and will usually avoid confrontation where possible.

The exceptions are if you accidentally corner an animal, surprise it at close quarters, or if the animal is injured or has young, in which case a mother will attack anything that she perceives as a threat.

Like the Chowgarh tiger, a large cat that has tasted human flesh before, usually due to an injury that prevents it from hunting its normal prey, may become a regular man-eater and a grave danger to those who live in the region.

Surprisingly though, it is the roly-poly hippo that accounts for more human deaths in Africa than any other animal; and the same can be said for the dopey-looking water buffalo in Southeast Asia.

However, sometimes things don't always go the hippo's way. During a military and scientific expedition in Zaire, a party was rafting down the foaming white waters in the Katanga gorges. Suddenly, the party came upon a hippo together with her calf in mid-river. The hippo took umbrage and charged. First, she bit the bow. On her second charge, she got the stern and finally she bit through what was left amidships. The Marines and scientists on board had prudently baled out into another craft. However, they were somewhat amused to look back at a very perplexed hippo that, having just eaten an inflatable boat, was suffering from terrible gas.

then led his father back to the village. His friends and family wanted to carry the man the 50 miles (80 km) or so to a hospital but he insisted that he wanted to die in his own home, convinced that he could not survive.

The villagers gave him water but it simply flowed out of the puncture holes in his neck.

The brave man was delirious for many days after. Remarkably, his wounds healed and he recovered fully, although he was horribly disfigured for the rest of his life.

There are very few people who can say they were attacked by a man-eater but survived. A brave man and a lucky escape, wouldn't you agree?

LEOPARD ATTACK

In South Africa in 1998, a rogue Kruger Park leopard ventured 6.2 miles (10 km) outside the park fence and attacked and injured villagers on their way to work.

First, the leopard attacked two brothers as they biked along a jungle track. It had Santos Chauke by the throat when his brother, Reason, started pelting the leopard with large stones. Next, it turned its attention to its tormentor. The leopard grabbed Reason by the left thigh and started to drag him off the road into the jungle. As he screamed, his brother, Santos, managed to get a small knife from his bag and stab the leopard in the hindquarters. Enraged, the leopard turned on Santos and started to attack him again.

LUCKY ESCAPE

For no apparent reason, the leopard then broke off its attack and bounded off into the bush.

Barely a few minutes later, Tinos Mkansi drove past in his bakkie (bus) with eight local villagers as passengers inside. He spotted the two abandoned bicycles and a large pool of blood and immediately stopped to see what had happened. Suddenly, the leopard leaped onto his windscreen, giving Mkansi the fright of his life, and then it jumped into the back of the bakkie among the passengers.

First, the leopard grabbed Lawrence Sihlangu by the shoulder before biting him in the face, neck, and torso. It also turned on the other screaming and fleeing passengers. The quick-thinking driver knew he had to do something to save Lawrence, so he grabbed a screwdriver from his cab and started to stab the leopard from behind.

LIFE-AND-DEATH STRUGGLE

The enraged leopard turned on Mkansi and the two struggled for 20 minutes before the leopard finally collapsed and died. Would you have risked your own safety to help a passenger or would you have run away like the others?

The returning passengers found the two Chauke brothers in the bush and loaded all the injured into the bakkie before rushing them to Matikwana Hospital for treatment.

Park rangers suggested the leopard must have

been deranged or sick to attack people in broad daylight in such a way.

Whatever the reason, I'd say that these men all showed remarkable bravery and selflessness to try to save another, wouldn't you agree?

Jungle Survivor's Tip

Surviving an Alligator Attack

Deaths in the United States from alligator attacks are rare, but there are numerous attacks and hundreds of fatalities from Nile crocodiles in Africa and from smaller crocs in Asia and Australia.

If you find yourself in the unfortunate position of being attacked by an alligator or crocodile, here's what you should do to wrestle free:

- If it attacks you on land, try to get onto its back and press down as hard as you can on its neck. This forces its head and, more important, its teeth down.
- Try to put some clothing or a rag over its eyes. This often has the effect of calming it down (mind you, I guess an angry crocodile is only marginally better than a furious crocodile).

• Strike at its eyes and nose first. Use any weapon you can lay your hands on and, if nothing comes to hand, use your fist.

• If the alligator has clamped its jaws on your arm or leg, tap or punch it on the snout. This provokes a reflex action and the alligator should open its mouth and drop whatever it is holding. Remember in Crocodile Dundee when the croc grabs the girl by the water bottle? Survival-trained Dundee punched it on the nose to release the bottle and then wrestled the croc himself, remember? — Well, you don't have to go that far but it's a good tip anyway.

• You must stop the alligator from shaking or rolling over with you because this causes terrible wounds. One way to prevent it from shaking is to keep the alligator's mouth clamped shut.

• If an alligator injures you in any way, however mild, seek immediate medical attention. If the bite doesn't kill you, the infection from the pathogens in its mouth will! And remember, steer clear of crocs and alligators wherever possible and keep your arms and legs inside boats when traveling in croc-infested waters.

A TALL TALE

There is a story that circulates around campfires in the jungle at night and the tale has been told and retold so many times that the original names have long been forgotten. However, once you've heard this chilling account, the image stays with you and you are always careful about where you sleep in the jungle.

A man fell asleep in his hammock in the jungle one night. During his sleep, one of his arms flopped over the side of his hammock and swung listlessly above the jungle floor.

When he awoke the next morning, a snake had swallowed the swinging arm and its massive head was up to the man's bicep. It would not loosen its grip, so the man's friends measured the length of his free arm and then measured the same distance plus a good few inches down the snake. They then chopped through the snake with an ax and the poor unfortunate man's arm was extracted from the dead snake's body.

A chilling warning to keep all your limbs in your hammock, I'd say!

Fact File

Although it should be stressed that large snakes rarely attack humans, it is not unheard of. In 1972, a python in Burma ate an eight-year-old boy and, in 2001, when hunters opened an anaconda that they'd caught and killed, a man was found intact in its stomach. It's believed the poor fellow was a woodcutter who had fallen asleep next to his woodpile and the huge snake had crushed him to death in his sleep and then gobbled him up whole. This is why big snakes such as pythons are not really suitable to be kept as pets. In 1993, in Colorado, a family's pet python attacked a 15-year-old boy weighing 95 pounds (43 kg). The snake was only medium-sized, about 11 feet (3.4 m), and weighing 53 pounds (24 kg), yet it was able to kill the boy, even though it made no attempt to eat him. Large snakes are fascinating and beautiful but they can be dangerous. And they don't have to live in the jungle to kill!

MILITARY RESCUES FROM THE JUNGLE

MILITARY RESCUES FROM THE JUNGLE

Search and rescue for a civilian survivor on foot in the vastness of the jungle is almost impossible unless your location is known or your downed aircraft has left a huge swath through the dense forests.

Yet, in the case of a military operation, where soldiers may find themselves in enemy territory, every effort must be made to extract survivors. Of course, military personnel are usually equipped with good communications equipment. And, if in the field on a mission, a rendezvous position will be prearranged.

Nonetheless, jungle rescues are perilous for both the rescuers and survivors alike, as you will see from our next bunch of amazing survival rescue stories.

BAT-21

The following is probably one of the most bizarre rescues of the Vietnam War.

On Easter Sunday, April 2, 1972, Colonel Iceal

Hambleton was flying as navigator in an American countermeasures aircraft, call sign Bat-21. The plane was over enemy territory in northern South Vietnam when it was struck by a surface-to-air missile (SAM). Col. Hambleton was the only man to eject safely, landing near a busy highway junction on an enemy supply route.

OVERWHELMING ODDS

Intelligence sources reported that the area contained 30,000 enemy troops. Initial attempts to rescue Col. Hambleton were frustrated by heavy ground fire.

Col. Hambleton was in contact with base through his survival radio that still worked despite submersion in water and other hardships – not bad, huh? – and this simple piece of equipment almost certainly saved his life.

A plan was devised to direct Col. Hambleton to a safer area where U.S. rescue planes could pick him up – it involved giving him directions by radio contact but, of course, the enemies who were also looking for Col. Hambleton could listen to these directions, too. So a cunning code was devised.

INGENIOUS PLAN

Col. Hambleton was an avid golfer and he remembered in great detail the courses where he had played, even down to the length of individual holes. A USAF reconnaissance aircraft photographed the area and photo analysts laid out a course for him to follow to a river 2 miles (3.2 km) away. To guide him safely past enemy camps, gun emplacements, and unfriendly villages, specific holes from certain golf courses were named, and from this the Colonel could establish the distance and direction of travel for each segment of his journey. This code made sense to golf-crazy Col. Hambleton but was complete nonsense to his Vietnamese eavesdroppers.

A DANGEROUS RENDEZVOUS

Traveling only at night, ten days had passed since he was shot down and Col. Hambleton was exhausted, having had nothing to eat or drink except several ears of corn and rainwater.

At the last "hole," he was met by Navy SEAL (Sea-Air Landing), Lt. Thomas R. Norris and a Vietnamese Ranger who had stolen a boat to meet him. Despite several enemy ambushes, they delivered Col. Hambleton to a waiting USAF helicopter, which took off under enemy fire.

A remarkable and resourceful rescue, wouldn't you agree? Although this was an extremely complex operation involving a good deal of technology and people – in fact, 234 medals were awarded to individuals for this rescue alone – it was good old-fashioned ingenuity, a reliable radio, plus a whole lot of courage and determination that saved the day.

Our next rescue was on a smaller scale, but it was no less daring or brave for that.

Fact File

The first Air Force helicopter rescue was made behind enemy lines in Burma on April 25 to 26, 1944. First Air Commando sergeant pilot Ed "Murphy" Hladovcak had crash-landed his plane with three wounded British soldiers on board. Taxing his helicopter to its limits, Lt. Carter Harmon made four flights to the site to rescue the men. On the final flight, he made a hasty liftoff just as shouting soldiers burst from the jungle. He later learned that the soldiers were not Japanese but an Allied land rescue party. I bet they were ticked off, don't you?

ESCAPE FROM ENEMY HANDS

A brutal civil war has raged for nine years in Sierra Leone, a mineral-rich West African country. In January 2000, Major Philip Ashby was part of a UN Observers team overseeing the fragile, newly established peace process. However, the respite from war was short-lived.

Ashby and his team were monitoring the disarming of the opposition rebel forces in the remote jungle and bush country of the

Northeast province. They had enjoyed some real success.

Yet, the good relations between the UN and the Revolutionary United Front (RUF), a rebel militia that violently opposed the government, was already starting to turn sour, and in May the RUF surrounded the camp where Ashby's UN observers and a garrison of Kenyan UN troops were based.

The UN observers tried to negotiate but the rebels captured and tortured their representatives. With great presence of mind, one of the negotiators, a Norwegian naval commander, put his radio on "transmit" so, while he endured terrible beatings and abuse, Ashby and his team could hear what was going on.

How brave was that!

In this way, they were tipped off that the rebels were forming a lynch mob for the UN troops in the camp.

A HARD DECISION

The garrison was manned by a mere seventy lightly armed Kenyan troops and they were greatly outnumbered by the rebels. Worse still, because of their neutral role, the fourteen UN observers were unarmed. Ashby asked the Kenyan sergeant major to find them weapons, but that would have meant disarming his own men, so he was unable to help. Can you imagine being a soldier and not being able to defend yourself? How awful!

Although the odds were heavily stacked against them, Ashby, two other British officers, and a New Zealander decided to try to escape.

Ashby was in contact with the UN headquarters via his satellite phone, and he asked permission to lead a group out of the siege but permission was refused. While the rebels taunted them and attacked the garrison, the Kenyan troops resisted as best they could and reluctantly the UN observers sat tight.

On the fourth day, Ashby heard from his British superiors. They believed he should try to escape. It was all the encouragement he needed.

Ashby and his three friends decided to head for a UN stronghold 50 miles (80 km) across rough bush and jungle. They took 1 quart (1 l) of water each, a 1962 survey map, a compass, a small first aid kit, a camera, and, of course, the heavy satellite (SAT) phone.

THE GREAT ESCAPE

In the dead of night, the four men slipped out of the camp. Sometimes, they would come across rebels and have to detour but they kept going. They struggled through bush, along a rebel-patrolled road, and up into hills covered with dense jungle.

Drenched in sweat and desperately thirsty, the group pressed on. Just before first light, they set up the SAT phone and sent a situation report. Then they hid themselves in the dense undergrowth and slept through the day.

Progress through the impenetrable jungle was desperately slow and morale was low. One of the officers was suffering from an unidentified tropical disease and they were all exhausted.

They decided to try to call for a helicopter pickup, but to their dismay, the battery on the SAT phone was drained. Unlike a military kit, SAT phones are not designed for being dragged through the jungle! But, can you imagine how desperately low they must have felt at that point?

THE LAST PUSH

Frantic to reach help, they decided to throw caution to the wind and to press ahead both day and night. They knew this policy would bring them into contact with local villagers and they prayed it would be someone sympathetic to them.

They put on their UN baseball caps and cautiously approached a farmer. They hoped to find a local guide who would know the jungle paths and could steer them clear of rebel-controlled villages. Through a combination of sign language and pointing, they were eventually directed to someone who spoke English.

Revived by freshwater and mangoes, the forlorn group was then led by a teenage local named Alusayne to a friendly militia, the Civilian Defence Force, or CDF for short. The CDF commander made them welcome and deployed ten of his men to guard them. The guards were armed only with machetes but they were determined to repel any RUF attack or attempt to get at their UN charges.

SOS MESSAGE

Soon some battered trucks arrived and the four survivors then faced a hairy 15-mile (24-km) ride through terrain held by the West Side Boys to reach the UN garrison. But, when they got there, their hearts sank. It was scarcely any better than the place they'd just escaped from! It was very remote, undermanned, and surrounded by hostile rebels occupying the neighboring villages. Out of the frying pan into the fire, you could say.

The one advantage was that this place had jeeps and they were able to use the jeep batteries to power up the SAT phone. However, because the troops still needed to use the vehicles, they could only power the SAT phone for eighty seconds of talk time. Who would you call in such a crisis?

They didn't want to be left hanging on the line by an operator, so eventually, Ashby decided to call his wife. A little while later, he managed to get a bit more power for the phone and he called his former boss in the UK, Colonel Babbington.

Remarkably, this marine commander told him that a helicopter would pick them up in fifteen minutes! This was a miracle because the nearest airport was at least an hour away. How could this be?

INTERVENTION

Later, they found out that the UK chain of command had identified their SAT phone signal and had triangulated their rough position. They'd listened in on Ashby's conversation with his wife, unbeknownst to either of them, and put up a helicopter immediately.

The next task for the UN observers was to persuade their militia friends not to open fire on the incoming helicopter.

The RAF Chinook helicopter touched down briefly and picked up the grateful men. Within an hour, they were all back at the International Airport near Freetown among friends.

EPILOGUE

Meanwhile, back at the compound from which they initially escaped, there were heavy casualties. After a week without water, the Kenyans had attempted a breakout but they were ambushed. Of Ashby's original team of observers, the three hostages were eventually released but they had all suffered brutal treatment and one had even lost a leg.

It seems Ashby's decision to break out was for the best, even though the experts only gave them a twenty percent chance of survival, at best!

Fact File

Jungle rescues by helicopter were pioneered in the Second World War and the art was perfected by the 10th Air Jungle Rescue detachment in Burma.

On one occasion, although Capt Charles Green, had crashed only a few minutes' flying time from an airfield, it took two weeks to rescue the severely injured pilot. Mainly, this was because combat engineers had to cut down trees, blast stumps, and level a crude hillside landing pad in thick jungle in order for the helicopter to make the hazardous pickup.

The funniest fact about this rescue is that Green crashed as a captain but was rescued as a major. He was promoted while waiting to be rescued!

THE PLACE OF THE DEAD

In 1994 in Borneo, a ten-man British army expedition led by Lt. Colonel Robert Neill attempted the first descent of a gully locals called the Place of the Dead. Otherwise known as

Low's Gully, it is a mile deep, bounded by sheer cliffs, and full of immense waterfalls, huge boulders, and dense jungle. It lies below the 13,435-foot (4,095-m) Mount Kinabalu, the highest mountain in Southeast Asia.

The expedition should have taken ten days to complete but two officers and three Hong Kong soldiers who were near to starvation were not plucked from the gully until almost a month after they set off.

DIVIDED THEY FALL

The party set off in good spirits but it soon became clear that there were huge disparities in the men's fitness levels and climbing abilities. The five faster men formed an advanced party and set off ahead of Lt. Col. Neill and the slower members of the group.

Unfortunately, Neill's party failed to make a rendezvous with the advance party and it was decided that they had no alternative but to press on. There was no turning back.

While climbing the vertical cliffs, one of the advance party, Cpl. Shearer was badly injured by a fall, and this again slowed the group. So, once more, the party split up, and L/Cpl. Mayfield and Sgt. Bob Mann went on ahead.

TERRIBLE INJURIES

While trying to hack his way through the impenetrable jungle, Sgt. Mann fell, slashing his hand deeply with a machete as he tumbled down the steep bank (he later underwent four operations). In the tropical heat, the wound quickly festered and became gangrenous.

The two men forged a strong bond in the face of such awful adversity. They huddled together in one sleeping bag for warmth at night and scraped the ubiquitous leeches off each other by day. They had no food, which had been left with the others in the advance party, and only the water from puddles to drink.

Each of the men buoyed the flagging spirits of the other. When Mayfield collapsed while climbing a cliff, it was Mann who pulled him to safety. Yet, four days before they escaped, Mann, weakened by his injury, begged Mayfield to leave him to die. But the marine would not leave his friend – he simply put his arm around his shoulders and made him carry on walking. Would you have stayed with your buddy, or would you have taken a chance to save your own bacon?

They kept telling each other, "We'll make it tomorrow," and it wasn't until after their ordeal that each confessed he had despaired of surviving at the time.

HELP AT HAND

On March 12, 1994, just as they were about to collapse from malaria and starvation, Mayfield and Mann crawled out of the Borneo jungle. Mayfield staggered to the nearest hut and started cramming rice from a cooking pot into his mouth. An old woman noticed Mann's gangrenous arm and made him plunge it into a liquid made from scorpions and molting snakes. Revolting as it sounds, this strange concoction almost certainly saved his arm from amputation.

The two were taken to a hostel to recover where they were later joined by the other three from the advance party who had also, miraculously, escaped from the jungle.

After raising the alarm to rescue Lt. Col. Neill and the others, Mayfield and Mann took the injured soldier, Cpl. Shearer, to the hospital.

The jungle nearly claimed the lives of all ten men and it was sheer grit and determination that got the advance party through and saved the lives of the whole party.

Pretty scary stuff, huh? Could you have carried on despite horrible injuries and disease or would you have given up and ended your days in the Place of the Dead?

SAVING LIVES

SAVING LIVES

It may sound ridiculous but the biggest threat to health in the jungle comes from our built-in fear of this strange and startling environment. In this teeming forest, you are constantly surrounded by the most weird and wonderful noises, and you can't see very much at all. Naturally, this can grate on the nerves and the general state of mind of any survivor.

Many jungle veterans report feelings of claustrophobia and panic attacks and unless you can get a grip on your fervent imagination before it runs away with you, you can end up defeating yourself before you even start.

Whether you're the sole survivor or one of a group, it's important that you have the right mental approach in the jungle. Be positive and don't let this unusual terrain intimidate you. Try to remember that of all the possible survival situations, the jungle provides the best in terms of food, water, and materials to make shelter, weapons, or transport.

If you can work with the jungle rather than trying to fight it, you'll find that life becomes easier. And with this positive, strong mental attitude, you're better placed to help yourself and others if some accident or illness befalls you.

SNAKEBITES

There are a lot of snakes in the jungle but most will not attack unless disturbed or provoked. Most snakes are shy and will do their best to avoid you, but if they do decide to strike, it happens with lightning speed. Whether it is you or a fellow survivor who is bitten, the important thing to remember is to stay calm.

If you're not certain whether a snake was poisonous or not, treat as though it were poisonous – although it may be easier to tell the casualty that it wasn't poisonous (yes, a white lie is OK in this situation) if you want to keep your patient calm!

Fact File
Of all the thousands of species of snakes, less than ten percent are dangerous.

TREATMENT

You're trying to prevent the poison from spreading through the body so keep the victim reassured and relaxed.

• Keep the bitten part of the body below the heart.

• Wash away any venom left on the skin, with soap if possible.

• Place a restricting bandage – NOT a tourniquet – above the bite, and bandage down over the bite. This prevents the toxin from spreading.

• If available, place the wound in cool water. (It's not applicable in the jungle, but if ice is available, use this.)

• You should treat the patient for shock and be aware that s/he may need artificial respiration.

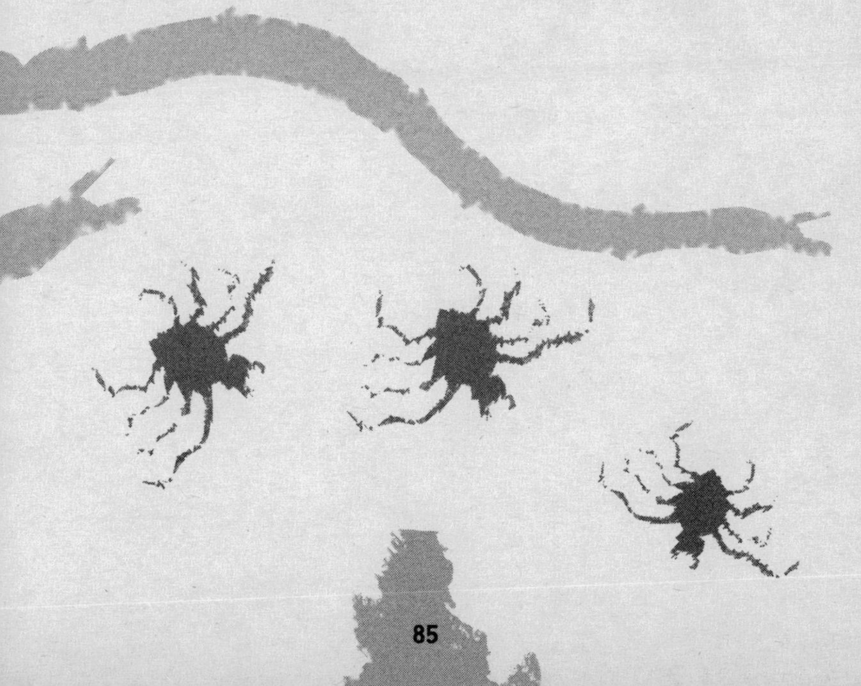

• Never cut a snake bite or try to suck out the poison – it's an old wives' tale that doesn't work.

• If, after fifteen minutes, the bite area is not painful or swollen and the casualty has no headache or dryness of the mouth, it's probably safe to assume that the bite was not poisonous.

Note: This same treatment applies for spider bites and scorpion stings.

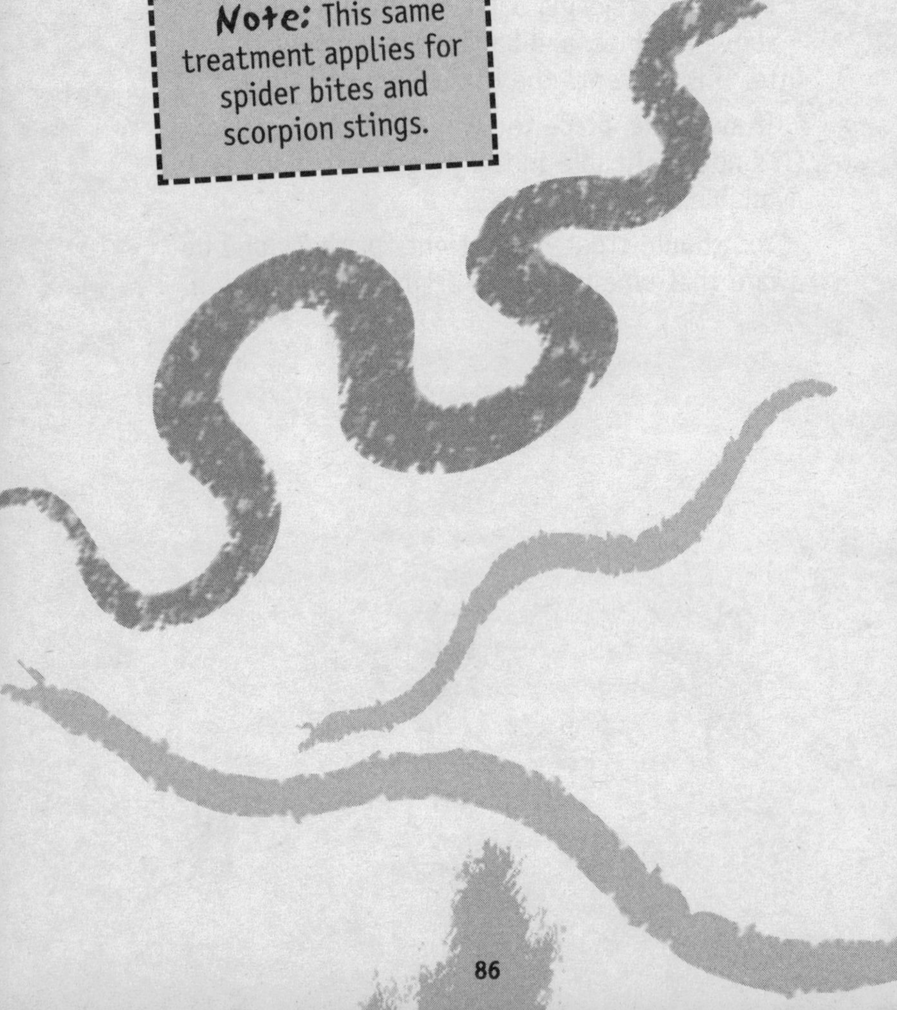

Fact File
The World's Biggest Snake
The largest known snake is the anaconda of South America. In 1944, a petroleum geologist recorded an anaconda measuring 37.5 feet (11.4 m) in length although there have been unproven reports of snakes much larger than this.
In fact, the explorer Col. Percy Fawcett himself described how he killed an anaconda that he estimated to be at least 62 feet (18.9 m) in length and with a diameter of 12 inches (30.5 cm). Locals in the Brazilian jungle have reported even larger specimens.
The anaconda lives in the freshwater rivers of the jungle and kills its prey by squeezing it to death. It loops its enormous body around an animal and each time the prey breathes out, it squeezes again until the animal can no longer breathe at all.

A horrible death, I'm sure you'll agree – did you see chapter five for some pulse-racing stories about surviving the less-friendly types of jungle wildlife?

HEAT EXHAUSTION OR STROKE

This is common in the jungle where every activity seems to take a great deal of energy and the humidity is exhausting.

SYMPTOMS

Heat exhaustion

Pale, cold skin, yet sweating, weak pulse, dizziness, cramps, delirium, and possibly bouts of passing out.

Heatstroke

Hot dry skin, a flushed and feverish face without sweating, high temperature, racing pulse, severe headache, vomiting, unconsciousness.

TREATMENT

- Get into the shade and raise the head and shoulders slightly.
- You can try fanning the patient or removing his or her clothes to cool him or her down.
- Make sure there is plenty of ventilation.
- When conscious, allow patient to sip water.
- Once his or her temperature has returned to normal, put his or her clothes back on, and keep warm.

Fact File

It may sound like some kind of cartoon ailment, but heatstroke is no joke. It can result in brain damage or even death. In July 1999, eighteen-year-old Claire Eisenegger from Surrey, England, died from heatstroke while on an expedition in the jungles of Borneo. Claire flew to the tropics to do some volunteer work in the summer before starting college to study medicine. Despite drinking a lot to avoid dehydration, Claire was working hard building jungle huts when she was taken ill with severe headaches and vomiting. After the alarm was raised and her condition stabilized in a makeshift medical center in the jungle, she was carried out of the jungle and taken by ferry to a hospital in Singapore. Sadly, she died thirty-five hours later in the hospital.

FUNGAL PROBLEMS

It sounds gross, doesn't it, but anyone who spends any time at all in the jungle will tell you that when your skin is constantly damp, the chances are that you'll end up suffering (and boy do you suffer) from some kind of fungal infection.

Unfortunately, unless you have some fungicidal cream with you, there's not a lot you can do. Athlete's foot (which affects the area between the toes, unsurprisingly), ringworm, and dhobi itch (which attacks the groin) are most common in the damp of the jungle and prevention is the best form of treatment. So, difficult though it may be, try to be very careful about personal hygiene in the jungle and wash every day.

SPRAINS AND BREAKS

In the jungle, sprains and broken limbs can be supported by a plant splint. Young palm trees make excellent splints, and a young banana tree is better still.

TREATMENT

- Find a young palm with a stem about 4 inches (10 cm) thick. Cut it off at the base and trim at the leaf end.
- Split and remove the outer layer and use the next inner layer of the same thickness as your splint.
- The splint should be long enough to cover the damaged limb and should be bound into place with vine or string.

- The peeled layer tends to grip the limb firmly and its inner coating has a pleasant cooling effect.

BITES AND STINGS

There are swarms of mosquitoes in the jungle that will drive you absolutely mad. They get everywhere (yes, even there!) and although the bites are furiously itchy, it is the fact that tropical mosquitoes carry dangerous diseases that is your biggest problem.

So, in this case, we'll look at prevention rather than treatment.

PREVENTION

- If you've got antimalarial drugs, take them as prescribed until your supply runs out.
- Mosquitoes breed in stagnant water so avoid making your camp near sluggish water or on swampy ground.
- Keep skin covered where possible. Tuck pants into socks and sleeves into gloves. If you don't have mosquito netting, improvise with parachute silk or even handkerchiefs – I'm sure you can come up with some good ideas.
- Use insect repellent if you have it. If not, smear exposed skin with mud, which can help deter less-determined mosquitoes. A smoky fire should keep most of the little pests at bay while at camp.

- Even the smallest creatures in the jungle seem to either bite or sting, unfortunately. The innocent little ant of our sidewalks at home has a far nastier cousin in the jungle. If disturbed, tropical ants will attack in swarms and they can inflict severe bites. The fire ant, in particular, can cause excruciating pain. Again, no real treatment suggestions but you are best advised to leave ants well alone.
- Bees, wasps, and hornets are also more aggressive in the jungle than they are at home. Keep your eyes open for nests, which can usually be spotted in trees about 10–30 feet (3–9 m) above ground.

TREATMENT

- Remove a lodged bee or wasp sting with tweezers, being careful not to squeeze the venom sac.
- Run or hold the area under cold water.
- Rub on soap or wash the area gently with vinegar or lemon juice.

LEECHES

The jungle is infested with leeches and they are particularly active after rain. They look just like small, black worms, and they attach themselves to you as you pass and then suck your blood until they're full.

Although the bite itself is more uncomfortable than dangerous, it does result in a loss of blood and it also opens the way for infection to enter the body. So make sure your pants are tucked into your boots when moving in the jungle and check every few minutes to see that leeches haven't attached themselves to you or your companions (teamwork is called for here!). At rest stops, check all over your body for leeches – they can end up in the most surprising nooks and crannies – behind your knees, under your armpits, around your genitals, and between your buttocks are some of their favorite haunts!

Jungle Survivor's Tip

Never put your face into the water to drink. A small leech may get into your mouth or stuck up your nose. If this happens, gargle or sniff up very salty water to get rid of it because they can cause serious infection in these areas.

TREATMENT

- If the leech has not latched on properly yet, you can just flick it away.

- If it has already bitten (you may not feel this as their saliva has anesthetic properties), do NOT try to pull it off. If you do, its jaws will remain embedded in your flesh and will cause infection.

• Instead, put salt or ash on it or approach it with a glowing ember (from fire or the tip of a cigarette if with a smoking adult survivor) and it will fall off.

• If you have access to unburned cigarettes, take the tobacco and place it in a cloth and moisten. Squeeze out onto the leech and it will loosen its hold.

• Clean the area by gently squeezing, allowing the blood to carry away anything nasty. After a while, the bleeding will stop and a scab will form. Leave this on for as long as possible to protect the wound from infection.

Jungle Survivor's Tip

Leeches will fall off naturally when they have had their fill of your blood.

WHAT
IF . . . ?

WHAT IF . . . ?

Are you one of those mindless types who are happy to do as you're told and go with the herd? Do you blindly follow someone else's lead without thinking about what you're doing?

No, I didn't think so for one minute. I can't believe that anyone interested in a book on survival is the type of person who never questions things or who has no ideas of their own.

So, I'm equally convinced that you'll also have your own very firm ideas on what is the best way to approach a problem. You may even be unwilling to listen to others' suggestions or laugh at them when they give it a try but get things wrong.

Well, neither extreme is right, I'm afraid. It's important in survival to be a team player, whatever the role you're playing. If you are in a party with an elected leader, then as long as you have faith in their judgment, you should follow their orders. Nonetheless, a good leader should accept constructive suggestions from members of his or her team, as long as it's not at moments of crisis when it's important for everyone to do as they are told without hesitation.

But, if you find yourself as a leader of a party or alone in a survival situation, you must rely on your own good judgment and cool head in a crisis.

I would add that it's never as easy to make

decisions in the field and under pressure as it is in theory but forewarned is forearmed, so giving a bit of thought to what you might do in a hypothetical situation is all to the good. Why not have a crack at these and see how you do?

A PERILOUS RIVER CROSSING

The plane that you and your friend were traveling in has crash-landed in the jungle. You are the only two survivors. You have taken some limited food provisions, a rope, matches, and an ax from the wreckage and you are attempting to walk out to safety.

The only thing that lies between you and a route to civilization is a fast-running river. It is too deep to wade across and too dangerous to attempt to swim (it's full of hungry piranhas and crocodiles and you're both bleeding from injuries sustained in the crash).

The tall trees come down close to the bank on your side of the river but it is relatively clear on the other side and you know a village is only a matter of 1 mile (1.6 km) or so beyond the other bank. Your provisions have run out and your strength is ebbing. This is your last chance to reach help.

How the heck are you going to get across? The answer lies in the scenario description itself (I must be going soft giving you clues) so give it a try and see what you come up with, OK?

RIVER CROSSING SOLUTION

So did you have any bright ideas? **I bet there were some brilliant ones!**

Some of you will probably have suggested building a raft, which isn't a bad idea. With the aid of the rope and a fixed point, you could probably get across the river but it's a lot of effort simply to cross the water. Also, with such a strong current, if the rope didn't hold, you'd be swept down river and could end up miles from your intended destination.

Did anyone come up with the idea of making a bridge? A+ to that smart cookie. You've got all the necessary equipment at your fingertips and with a bit of effort, you'd be across in no time at all.

For those of you who had the idea but didn't quite know how to put it into practice, here's the experts' inside info on how to build a bridge.

BUILDING A BRIDGE

Cut down two or three long straight trees and trim off any obtrusive branches.

Attach the ropes to the far end of one log and you and your friend stand on either side with a rope each.

Peg a short log into the ground by sticks to chock the near end and stop it sliding back, then lower the log across the river.

With the first log in place, slide a second log along it until the end reaches the opposite bank.

Roll the second log off the first one onto the bank. Try to keep the logs close together.

You can now shinny across the logs to the far side.

If you wanted to make a more permanent bridge, when you reach the other side, put a short log under the logs' ends to prevent them from sinking into the ground.

Peg the logs in place so they don't spread apart and do the same at the other end.

You can make your bridge as wide as you like but three logs are usually enough.

Jungle Survivor's Tip

Crossing Water

If forced to wade across water, do so fully clothed.

Check water for hazards such as crocodiles and caymans — in 2000, in Peru, a Ph.D. student dived from the research center into a lake to cool off at dusk and was taken by a black cayman that was 20 feet. (6 m) in length.

Steer clear of shallow waters in the dry season — these may house schools of piranhas.

Cut a stick to aid balance.

Cross facing towards the current and you're less likely to be swept off your feet.

Always keep your boots on — they'll give you a better grip than bare feet.

Undo the belt fastening of a backpack so you can slip it off easily if you get swept over.

Shuffle rather than stride, using the stick to test for depth, and try each foothold before using it.

Fact File

There is a tiny 1-in (2.5-cm) long Amazonian fish called the Candiru that is reported to swim up the most sensitive part of the male anatomy when urinating in water. Once inside, its back-folded dorsal fin acts as a barb, causing excruciating pain and a serious medical problem. I suggest you remember this next time that you're tempted to pee in the water while wading across an Amazonian river!

MAYDAY – DOWNED AIRCRAFT – MAYDAY

Your light, fixed-wing aircraft has crashed in the jungle and you have been knocked unconscious by the crash-landing. When you come around, you realize that you are virtually unharmed but the pilot has been killed.

Unfortunately, your plane is caught up high in the canopy some 100 feet (30 m) above the jungle floor. The door has been ripped off the small plane and your position is rather precarious. You need to get down, but how?

Any ideas?

CRASHED PLANE SOLUTION

The most obvious answer is to try to climb down and I wouldn't blame any of you for coming up with that one. However, in the jungle, the branches of a tree will probably run out before you reach the ground and you will still be dangerously high.

A fall from a high tree will almost certainly mean severe injury if not death, so you must proceed with caution.

First, search the plane for any items that may be useful in your survival situation – survival packs, rations, tools, etc. – and drop them to the ground before you leave the plane.

Find a rope (usually on board) or knot together parachutes and attach the rope to a strong branch before dropping it to the ground (make sure it reaches before setting off).

If there are lowering devices such as karabinas and figure-of-eights on board, so much the better. Most pilots who are active over the jungle carry this equipment. However, if not, hold the rope around your waist and over one shoulder as you lower yourself down. Attach yourself to the rope using cargo webbing.

Wear gloves if possible. If not available, wrap your hands in rags or bandages before setting off.

KILLER BEES

It's a hot, humid afternoon as you hack your way through the undergrowth following the route of the river towards a village. Suddenly, you hear a droning that gets louder and louder. When you look behind you, you realize that your crashing about in the foliage has disturbed a nest of angry bees in the tree above.

The swarm of aggressive bees is leaving the nest and looking for trouble. What in heaven's name are you going to do? Have you got any clues?

KILLER BEES SOLUTION

The stings of tropical bees and hornets can be fatal in large numbers and these species are particularly aggressive, so you're really in hot water here. What did you decide was the best course of action?

Well, surprisingly, if the bees are swarming but not attacking you, the best advice is to stay very still, preferably sitting, and not move for at least five minutes. Once the worst threat has passed, crawl away slowly and carefully.

On the other hand, if the swarm attacks you, staying put is the last thing you should do. Get out of there as quickly as possible. Run through the densest foliage you can find – the branches should spring back after you to beat back and/or confuse the insects. Don't swat at the bees around your body, this will only make them angrier and they will sting any exposed flesh they can find.

The other option is to jump into the water (remember, I said you were walking by the river?) and stay submerged for as long as possible. But be warned – bees have been known to wait for their victim to surface and then attack again.

Did you get that solution? Let's hope so.

Jungle Survivor's Tip

If you have to jump into water from a height, make sure you use the right technique:

- Jump in feetfirst. NEVER dive into unknown water — you could be killed or disabled if you hit your head on submerged rocks.
- Keep your body completely upright.
- Squeeze your legs and feet together and clench your bottom.
- Check that you will land in deep water before jumping.
- After entering the water, spread your arms and legs wide and "scull," which will slow down your descent and help you to resurface.

JUNGLE SURVIVOR'S BRAIN-TEASERS

JUNGLE SURVIVOR'S BRAINTEASERS

One of the first rules of survival is staying calm and being prepared. So, if from the comfort of your own home you've already given some thought to what you might do to help yourself in certain survival crises, you're already ahead of the game.

The following training exercise is something of a puzzler – and, admittedly, somewhat unlikely in this day and age, although cannibalism in Papua New Guinea was a reality as recently as forty years ago!

If you find it hard to figure out, you might find it easier to play out the scenario. Sometimes it becomes clear when you put a theory into practice and, as long as you don't bicker, several heads can be better than one.

So, get a group of your buddies together and assign each a role as either an explorer, a paddling, or a non-paddling cannibal. Using piggyback to simulate crossing the river by canoe, act out your solution and see if it works. If it doesn't, the cannibals have my permission to eat the explorer left on their bank!

With that thought in mind, you may as well get started.

EXPLORERS AND CANNIBALS

It is the early 1960s and you and two friends are exploring in the Yominbip area of Papua New Guinea. Trouble is brewing in the region and you realize that your lives are in danger. You have to escape without delay. Unfortunately, you are not familiar enough with the area to travel alone and so you have to rely on three local guides to lead you to safety. However, you know these men come from a tribe of people who eat their enemies.

Your party of six, three explorers and three cannibals, set off to find the airstrip and safety. Suddenly, you are faced with an obstacle. You must cross a fast-flowing, crocodile-infested river using a two-person canoe. The problem is that although all three explorers can canoe skillfully, only one of the cannibals has this skill.

RULES

No swimming is allowed and rope is not available to tow the boat back and forth. If you leave the explorers outnumbered on either bank, the cannibals will eat them. How can you cross in such a way as to get everyone over without sacrificing any of you explorers?

SOLUTION

So, did you manage to figure it out? Tricky, isn't it? Personally, I always find it easier to act these scenarios out but you don't always have the luxury in a real survival situation so you have to be able to analyze the situation and come up with the best solution possible while thinking on your feet.

Anyway, for those of you who've found yourselves eaten by your friends more times than you care to mention, here is the answer.

There are probably several ways in which this can be done but the simplest is to get the paddling cannibal to ferry everyone across. First he takes an explorer. Then he comes back for a cannibal. Next he takes another explorer and then he returns for the final cannibal. At no time is there a ratio of less than one explorer to one cannibal, so everyone is safe although the poor paddling cannibal might be a bit tired by the end of it all!

It's easy when you know how, isn't it!

And finally . . .

It's become something of a tradition in my survival books to leave you at the end of this chapter with a stinker of a brainteaser. So, if you want to flex your mental muscle, here goes.

While you're staying in an Indian village in the jungle, you adopt three stray dogs and start to feed them. You reckon that a dog and a half need a bone and a half in a day and a half. So how many bones does one dog need in six days?

Don't cheat by looking at the answers unless you're really stumped. I trust you to be honest now!

SOLUTION

Three dogs will need three bones in the time ($1\frac{1}{2}$ days), which is an average of one bone per dog. Since six days is four times $1\frac{1}{2}$, a single dog would need FOUR bones. Simple (unless, like me, you're no good at math!).

YOUR JUNGLE SURVIVOR'S RATING

YOUR JUNGLE SURVIVOR'S RATING

I know time flies when you're enjoying yourself, but it scarcely seems possible to me that we've come to the end of our journey together. It's been fun and I hope you've enjoyed the ride.

Before we go our separate ways (and before you think I'm just a regular nice guy), there's one last rotten test for you to undertake. Think you're up to it?

Well, this final quiz will sort the great from the good, so let's see how much jungle savvy you've picked up along the way, shall we?

1. An anaconda, the world's biggest snake, kills its prey by:

A rearing up and spitting venom in its eyes
B biting and injecting venom into its bloodstream
C squeezing the life out of it
D breaking its neck with its powerful jaws

2. To keep crawling insects from your sleeping area at night, what should you spread around you?

A ash
B honey
C water
D fire

3. One of the best supplies of freshwater can be found in plants. The vine is particularly useful. To obtain water:

A cut the bottom of the vine and wait for it to run out

B cut the top of the vine and suck

C cut the top of the vine and then the bottom and allow the water to drip from the top

D cut the vine into segments and wring out

4. In primary jungle, trees can grow:

A over 33 ft (10 m) high

B over 67 ft (20 m) high

C over 134 ft (40 m)

D over 200 ft (61 m) high

5. If you are going to signal for help, the best method is:

A permanent ground signals left in a clearing

B a signal fire in the trees

C a whistle

D a message in a bottle

6. To remove a leech from your body, you should:

A yank it off
B touch it with a glowing ember
C leave it to fall off
D ask it nicely to leave

7. As you walk past a waterhole, a huge crocodile clamps its jaws around your leg and starts to pull you towards the water. What should you do to save yourself?

A pry its jaws apart with a stick
B lie still and play dead
C blow in its nostrils
D punch it hard on the nose

8. To escape a ferocious jaguar attack, you have to jump 40 feet (12 m) into a river from a high outcrop of rock. Should you:

A roll up into a tight ball
B dive headfirst
C squeeze your legs together, clench your bottom, and jump
D belly flop

9. You have stepped into quicksand and are sinking rapidly. What should you do?

A spread your arms and legs wide and try to float on your back
B flail your arms and legs about in an attempt to reach firmer ground
C take your shoes off
D pray

10. When choosing a good spot to set up camp for the night, you should choose:

A a swamp
B a dry watercourse
C an animal trail
D high ground

11. When Sgt. Mann staggered from the Borneo jungle, a local woman put his gangrenous hand in a potion made from:

A maggots and leeches
B snake venom and poison
C scorpions and moulting snakes
D jaguar dung and snake blood

12. Before setting off to travel through the jungle, you should prepare yourself by wearing:

A shorts and a t-shirt to stay cool
B sunblock plus a hat that covers the back of your neck
C long-sleeved tops and pants that are loose fitting
D waterproof clothing

ANSWERS

1c An anaconda is a constrictor, which means it wraps its powerful coils around its prey and literally squeezes the life from it. Actually, because the anaconda lives in the water, it often winds up drowning its victims as they are pulled into the river. Either way, it's not a pleasant end, is it?

2a For some unknown reason, creepy crawlies don't like slithering over ash, so putting a ring around your sleeping area and kit is a good deterrent. Honey would draw beasties to you in the jungle quicker than anything and digging a moat around yourself is simply not worth the effort. I hope none of you chose a ring of fire around your bed – think about it.

3c Did you get in a muddle over this one? If you remember that the vine works by capillary action, you'll remember that water is pumped up the plant, so cut the top first and then the bottom to allow it to come out.

4d Yep, these giants can grow to over 200 feet (61 m) high. That's a long way to drop if you're hung up in the canopy by your parachute or in a crashed, light aircraft, don't you think?

5a Rescue will probably come from the air and the first place a rescue aircraft will search is in clearings and along riverbanks. Sadly, smoke from signal fires cannot be seen because of the sheer density of the jungle canopy – and if you think a whistle will get you anywhere, you must be completely mad. I suppose a message in a bottle might be found but you'd have to have time on your side and just pray whoever finds it reads English.

6b Yep, as you've seen in all the best action movies, leeches will drop off if you apply an ember to them. Never try to pull them off. If you do, their jaws will remain embedded in your flesh and will get infected. You could wait for them to drop off once they are full but if they are on your body in any number, you'll be severely weakened by the blood loss, so it's not a good idea. Good manners don't cost anything, but I doubt they'll get you anywhere in the jungle.

7d A reflex action makes a crocodile or alligator open its mouth and drop what it's holding when it's hit hard on the snout. At least, that's the theory. A crocodile's jaws are immensely strong, so it would be futile to try to pry them open. Lie still and play dead and you very soon will be! And as for blowing in its nostrils? You're thinking of a horse-whisperer, you dingbat.

8c You're going to hit the water at a high speed so you want to prevent water from being forced under pressure into your private nooks and crannies. If you went for any of the other options, it's going to hurt like hell, so good luck.

9a Quicksand is rather like dense water – you can float on it and then gradually work your way to the side. Frantic wriggling will only result in you sinking faster, and taking your shoes off is of no benefit whatsoever. Praying for divine intervention might make you feel better and maybe even calmer, but you have to help yourself, too, in a survival situation.

10d All of the other choices will get you into difficulties with the local wildlife, whether it be marauding mosquitoes or terrifying tigers. You're definitely safest on high ground, if you don't want to be attacked or washed away.

11c Yes, gross though it sounds, the potion was made from scorpions and molting snakes, although all the other combinations sound equally far-fetched to me.

12c You need to cover up against the inevitable insect bites and scratches from thorny vegetation. Funnily enough, because of the dense foliage, protection against sunburn is not normally necessary and the humidity makes waterproof gear a waste of time, as it will simply make you sweat.

So, how did you fare? Are you a bit of a Tarzan, Lord of the Apes, the greatest jungle survivor of all time, or more of a Mowgli, the man-cub with lots still to learn? I trust it's the former but, if you didn't get a brilliant score, never fear, there's always plenty of room for improvement.

And, believe me, even the most seasoned survival experts can still learn a new trick or two. Survival is a never-ending learning curve and everyone has to start somewhere. As for the jungle, once you grow accustomed to this startlingly strange environment, you realize that you really couldn't pick a better or more astounding place to start your survival education.